The First Song Ever Sung

BY **LAURA KRAUSS MELMED**

ILLUSTRATED BY **ED YOUNG**

LOTHROP, LEE & SHEPARD BOOKS   NEW YORK

First Edition   1   2   3   4   5   6   7   8   9   10

Library of Congress Cataloging in Publication Data
Melmed, Laura Krauss. The first song ever sung / by Laura Melmed ;
illustrated by Ed Young.
    p.   cm.   Summary: Animal and human friends provide lyrical
answers to a young boy's musical query. ISBN 0-688-08230-0.—
ISBN 0-688-08231-9 (lib. bdg.)   [1. Songs—Fiction. 2. Bedtime—
Fiction.]   I. Young, Ed, ill.   II. Title.   PZ7.M51627Fi   1992
    [E]—dc20   91-28628   CIP   AC

to Jonathan, who asked the question

—LKM

to "the gardeners of the spirit who know that without darkness
nothing comes to birth as without light nothing flowers" — (ANON)

—EY

"What was the first song ever sung?"
said the little boy to his father.

"The first song ever sung was a strong song,
a man's song, a warrior's song, a friend's song,"
said the father to the little boy.

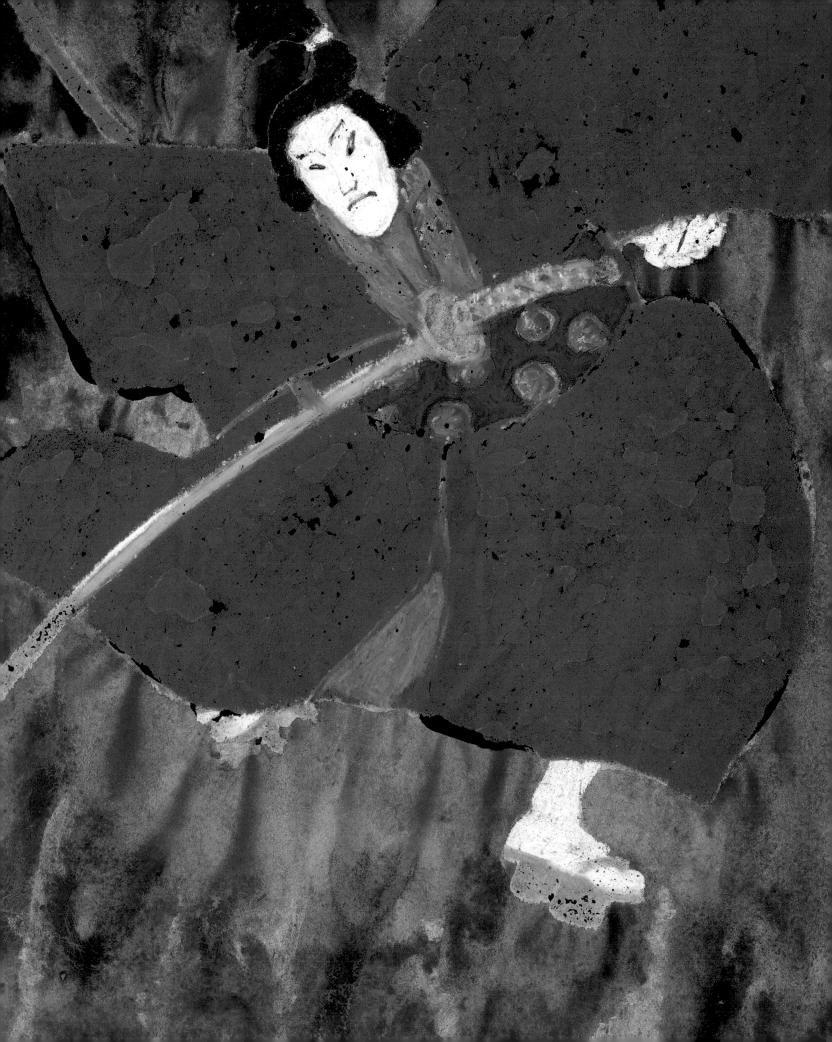

"What was the first song ever sung?"
said the little boy to his brother.

"The first song ever sung was a proud song,
a loud song, a stomping, shaking, shout song,"
said the brother to the little boy.

"What was the first song ever sung?"
said the little boy to his sister.

"The first song ever sung was a rope song,
a swing song, a jumping, twirling, leap song,"
said the sister to the little boy.

"What was the first song ever sung?"
said the little boy to his grandmother.

"The first song ever sung was a spinning song,
a weaving song, a magic thread and thimble song,"
said the grandmother to the little boy.

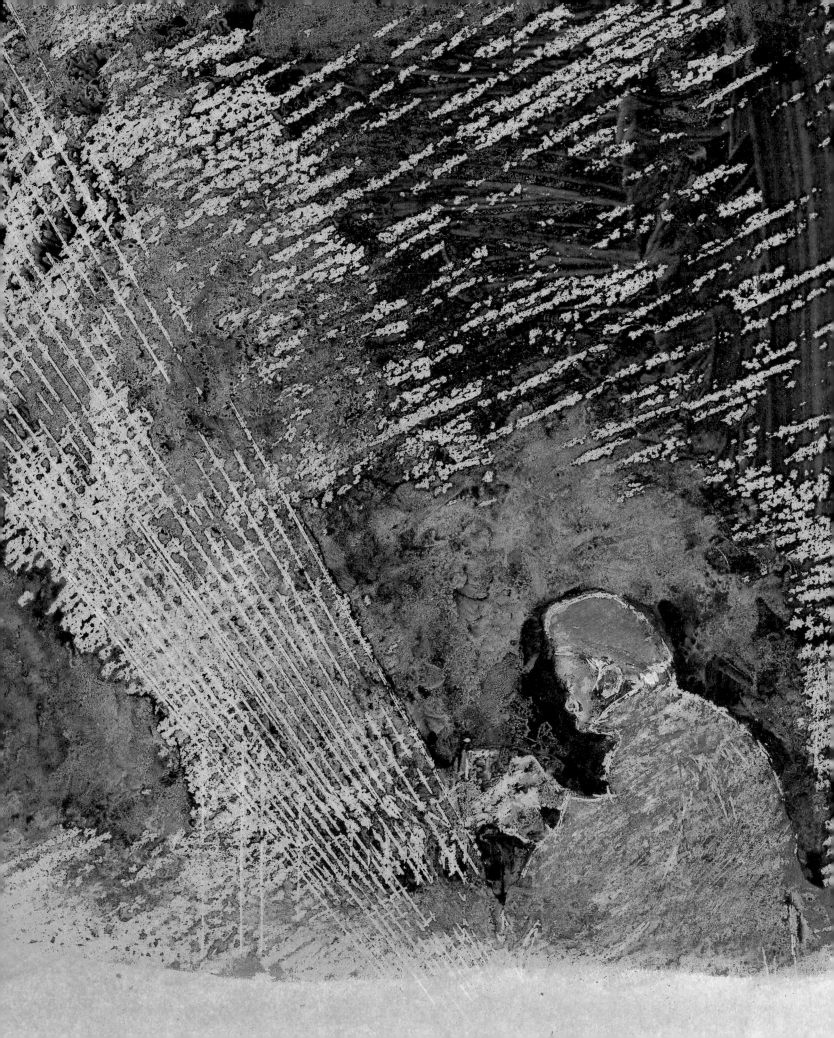

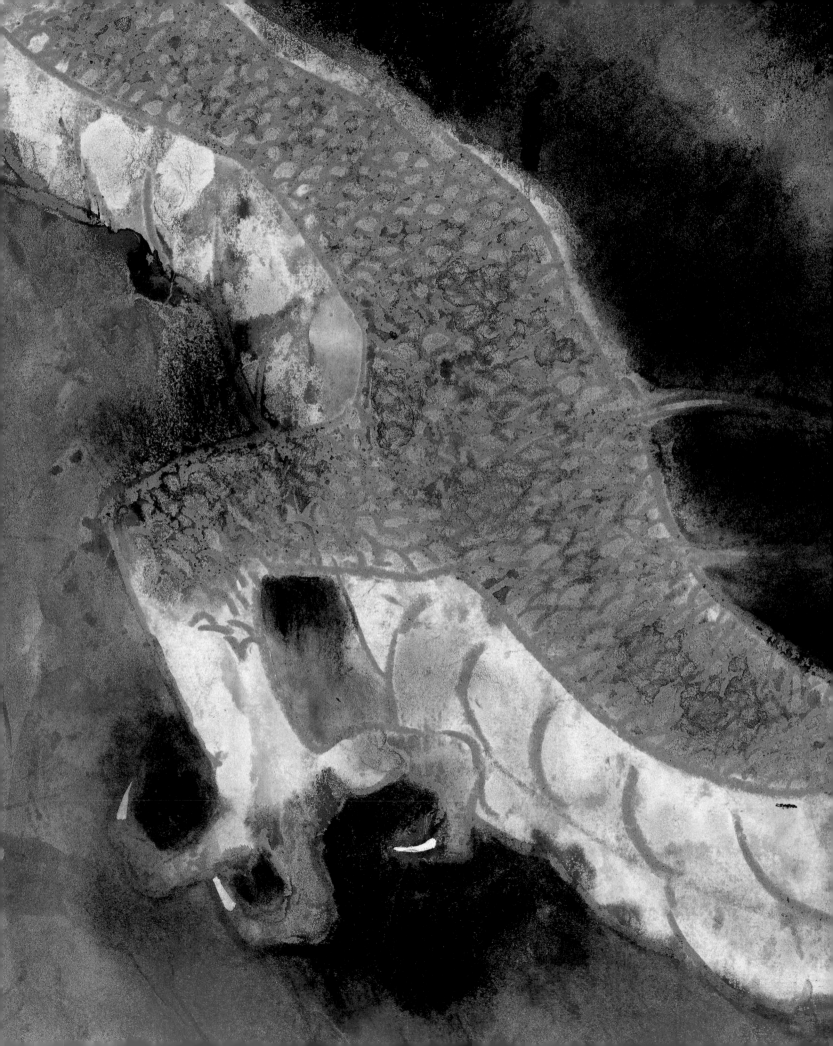

"What was the first song ever sung?"
said the little boy to his grandfather.

"The first song ever sung was a seed song,
a sprout song, a rain song, a harvest song,"
said the grandfather to the little boy.

"What was the first song ever sung?"
said the little boy to his dog.

"The first song ever sung was a moon song,
a howl song, a lone song, a bone song,"
said the dog to the little boy.

"What was the first song ever sung?"
said the little boy to the minnows in the brook.

"The first song ever sung was a ripple song,
a splash song, a pebble song, a flash song,"
said the minnows to the little boy.

"What was the first song ever sung?"
said the little boy to the birds in the sky.

"The first song ever sung was a sing song,
a wing song, a dawn song, a dream song,"
said the birds to the little boy.

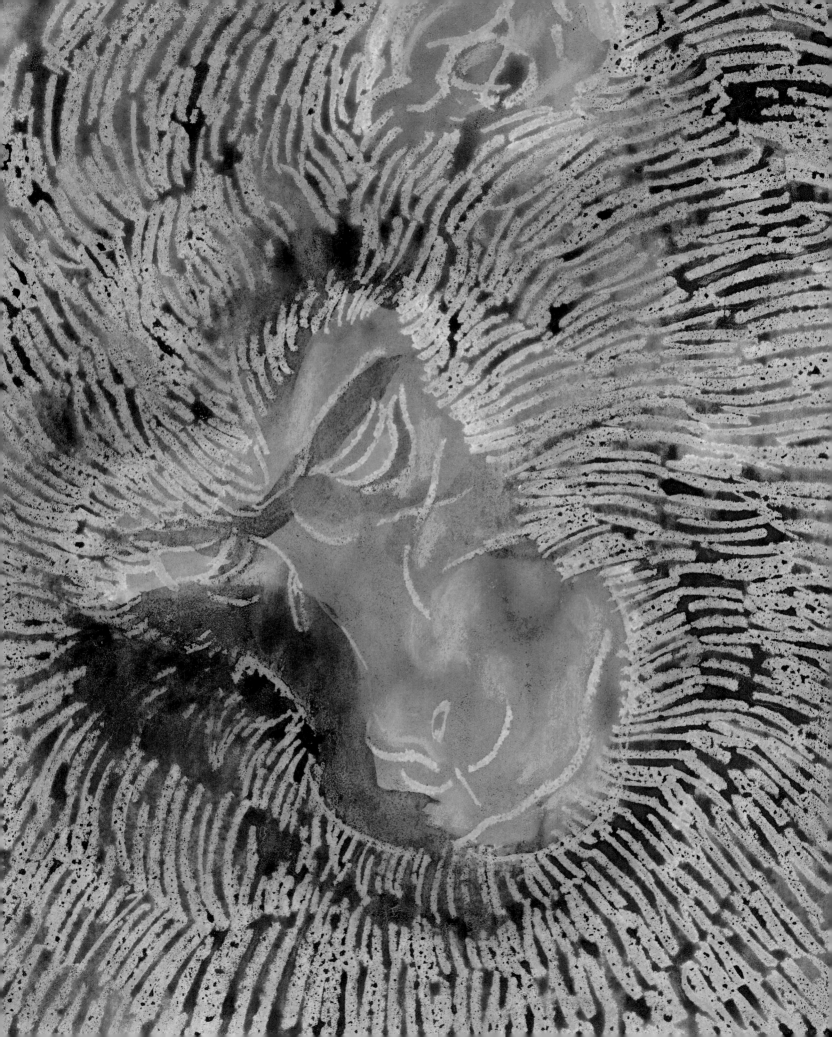

"What was the first song ever sung?"
said the little boy to his mother.

"The first song ever sung was a mother's song,
a hush song, a sleep song, a love song,"
said the mother to the little boy
as he climbed into her lap.

And she sang him gently to sleep.